To Newenka, a cyclist, an explorer, and a true friend

Gold medal winner of
the Key Colors Competition USA, 2022

The New Bicycle written and illustrated by Darcy Day Zoells

ISBN 978-1-60537-964-7

This book was printed in December 2023 at Dream Colour Printing Company Limited 101,
Building A006, Zhiji Group, №92, Jinye Road, Kuixin Community Kuichong Street,
Dapeng New District, Shenzhen City, Guangdong Province, China.

First Edition
10 9 8 7 6 5 4 3 2

THE NEW Bicycle

NEW YORK

Darcy Day Zoells

Mari's new bicycle was bigger, bolder, and brimming with possibilities.

When she pedaled fast, her new bicycle nearly flew.

The bell on the handlebars seemed to sing "hello!"

Mari's new bicycle had *two* baskets!
The front carried little loads, but the back could handle even more.

Now Mari could carry almost anything.

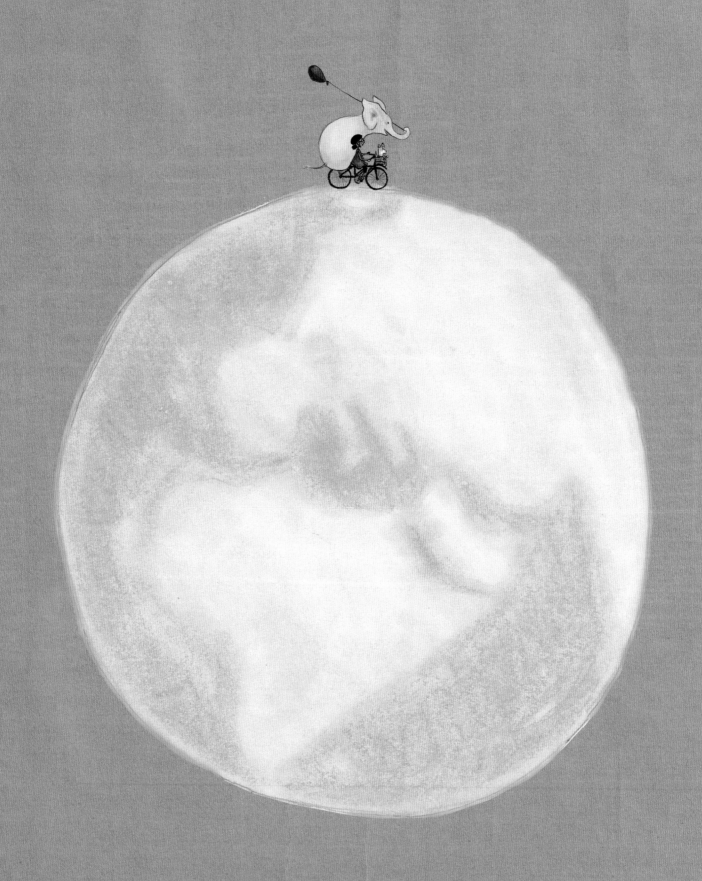

And go almost anywhere.

Mari could follow the path no matter where it led, even all the way to . . .

. . . the end . . .

. . . and beyond!

On her new bicycle, Mari could make her own way.

New ways could lead to new friends.

And new places to explore.

Mari could make discoveries and deliveries.

Her new bicycle could take her far.

But it could do something even more important.

Mari's new bicycle could always bring her home.